DREAMWORKS
DRAGONS
Doodle Book

D1472392

DREAMWORKS
PRESS
Los Angeles * New York

The first picture Tron remembers drawing is a boat. His dad saved his drawing in a book for many years.

It's not a race to see who can draw the fastest. It's about enjoying what you're doing.

Celebrate being yourself and don't worry about fitting in. Individuality creates interesting characters.

Meet Tron Mai.

Tron is a story artist at DreamWorks Animation. He worked on the movie *How to Train Your Dragon 2*, but Tron started drawing long before the Island of Berk and Toothless. He sketched and drew the world around him, just like you!

Check out Tron's workspace and read his tips for doodling your best doodles. Just remember his most important advice: have fun and let loose!

When he was a kid, Tron would go to the library and find pictures that he wanted to draw.

Especially for Conner

Written by Samantha Suchland
Illustrated by Tron Mai

Dragons Doodle Book © 2015 DreamWorks Animation Publishing, LLC.
How To Train Your Dragon 2 © 2015 DreamWorks Animation LLC.

First Edition
Printed in China
10 9 8 7 6 5 4 3 2 1
ISBN 978-1-941341-17-9
04012015-F-1
Visit dreamworkspress.com

DreamWorks
Artist's Corner

Tron draws sketches in a sketch book before drawing on his computer.

Tyler and Tucker are Tron's dogs. They run around his office and inspire him when he is drawing characters like the dragon, Toothless.

Flip Book Instructions

Included in this book are TWO flip books for you to doodle. The one on the right side of page is finished. And the one on the left side is for you to complete all on your own.

Flip books are a sequence of pictures that slowly change from one page to the next and when the pages are turned, the pictures appear to move. Sort of like a little movie made of out paper, pencil, and marker.

Here's how to do it:

1. Think about how the animation (picture) will look on each page of your flip book. For example, if you decide that you want a dragon flying, the first frame (or page of the flip book) shows the dragon spreading its wings, the next frame shows the dragon beginning to lift off the ground, the next frame shows the dragon flying up to the sky, and the next page has the dragon in a different spot in order to show movement.

2. Sketch your animation on each page with a pencil. This way, you can easily erase or make changes to your drawing.

3. It's really important that each picture is slightly different than the last one. This way, when the pages are turned quickly (by flipping the pages) the picture appears to be moving. Bigger changes will appear as faster movement when you flip. Smaller changes will seem slower.

4. Flip through the book occasionally as you draw to make sure that the drawings on each page animate smoothly.

5. Go over the outlines with a marker when you are finished. You can also used colored markers.

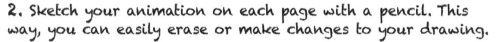

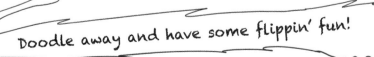

Doodle away and have some flippin' fun!

Welcome to Berk, where Vikings live
alongside dragons.
Draw yourself as a Viking.

Good morning, dragons! Today's the big race.

Draw the waking dragons.

Vikings wear lots of layers and
fur because it's cold in Berk.

Draw the Viking's clothes.

Vikings don't fight dragons anymore. Now they race!

Draw racing stripes
on this dragon.

The Dragon Racers compete to collect the most sheep before the race ends.

Draw patterns on each sheep.

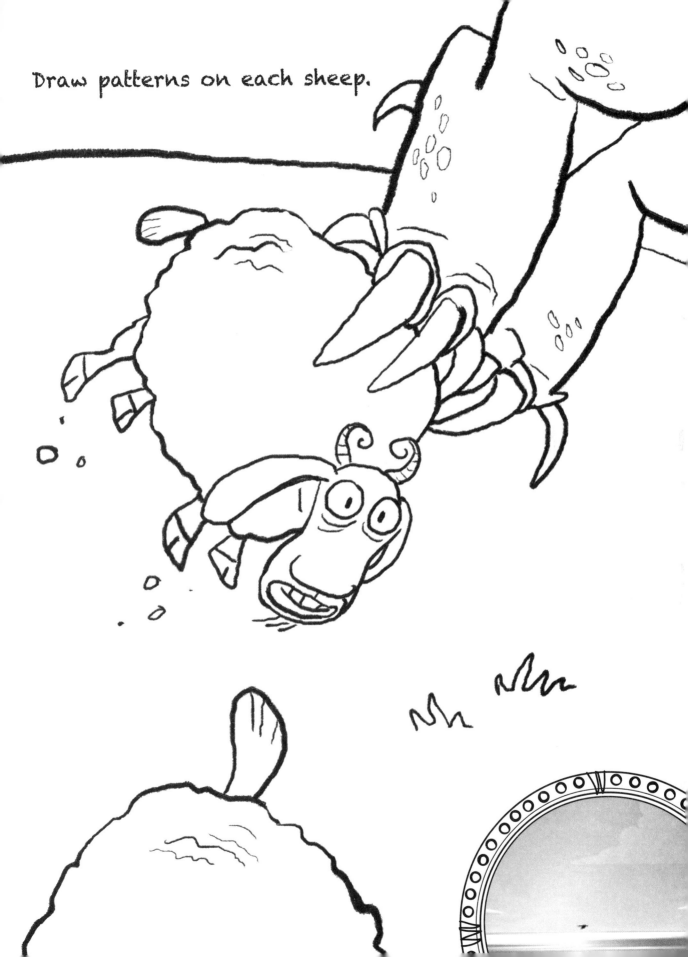

The Vikings have flags and banners
for their favorite Dragon Racer.

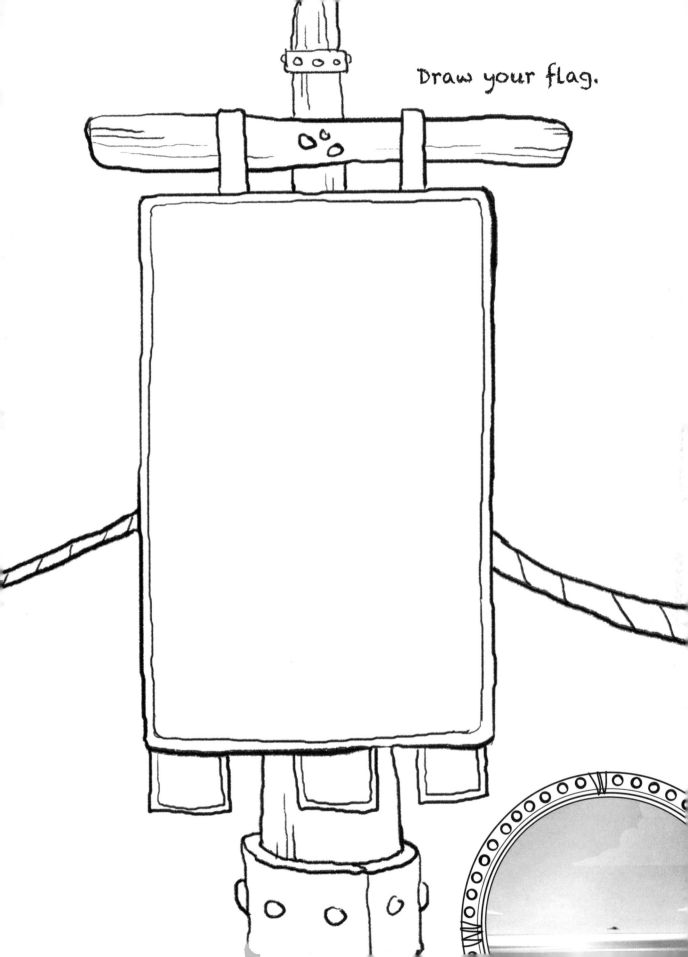

Draw your flag.

The Vikings cheer on the Dragon Racers from the stands.

Finish the crowd.

Dragon Racers swoop and dive through obstacles. Flying upside down is a great way to steal sheep from other racers.

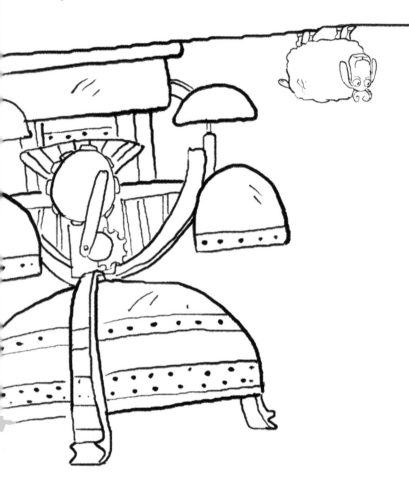

Draw Berk upside down.

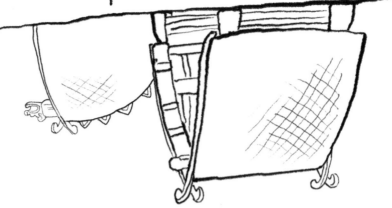

Astrid has the most sheep going into the final lap.
Her net is almost full!

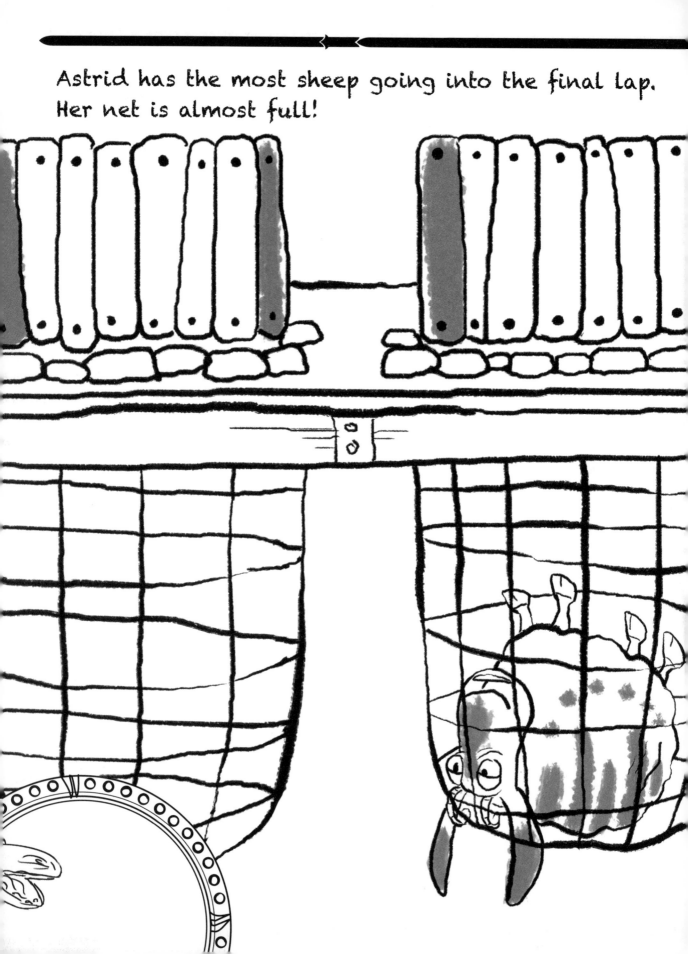

Draw Astrid's sheep.

The black sheep is worth more points than all the others. Where is he hiding?

Draw the black sheep.

Draw your dragon on the podium.

Draw your prize.

Hiccup missed the Dragon Race. He is busy exploring the world beyond Berk.

Finish Hiccup's map.

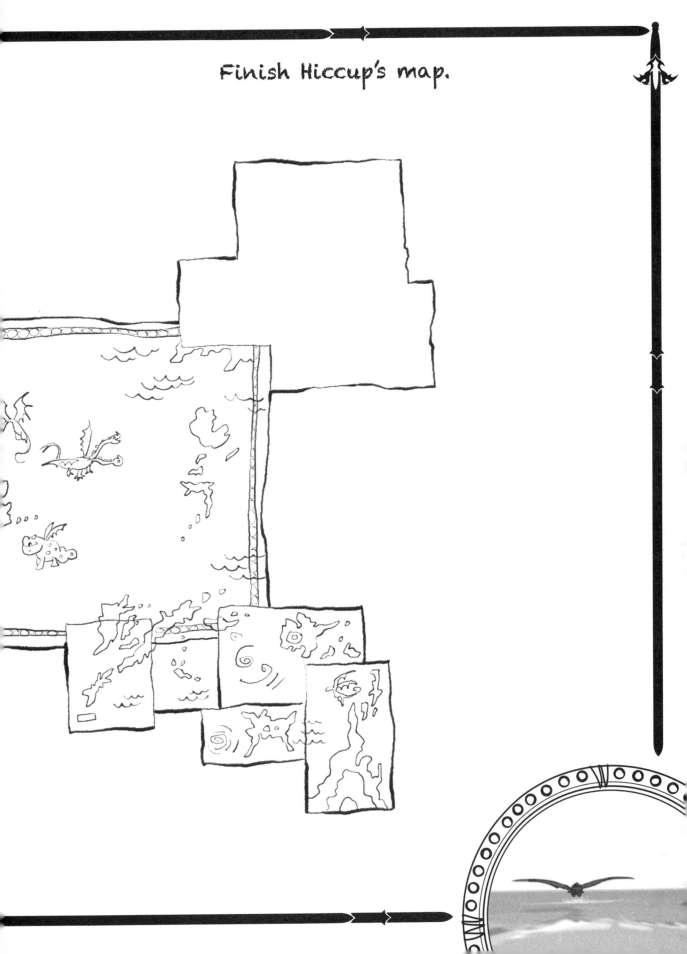

Toothless helps Hiccup discover a
new land called Itchy Armpit.

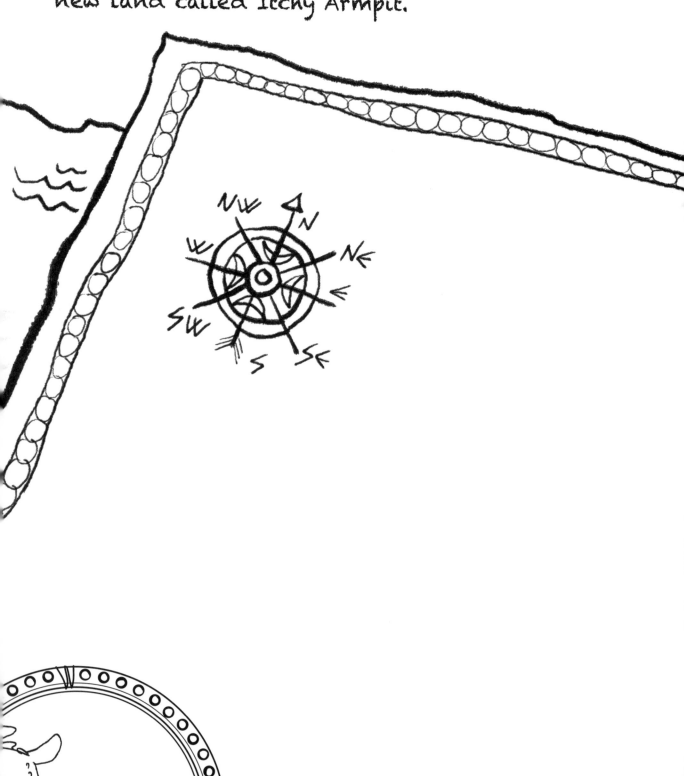

Draw Itchy Armpit.

Hiccup and Toothless teach the Vikings how to live with dragons.

Draw a dragon for each Viking.

The Vikings of Berk don't worry about dragons starting fires. They are prepared with big buckets filled with water.

Draw the fire.

Gobber makes custom Dragon
Riding saddles at his workshop.

Draw your saddle.

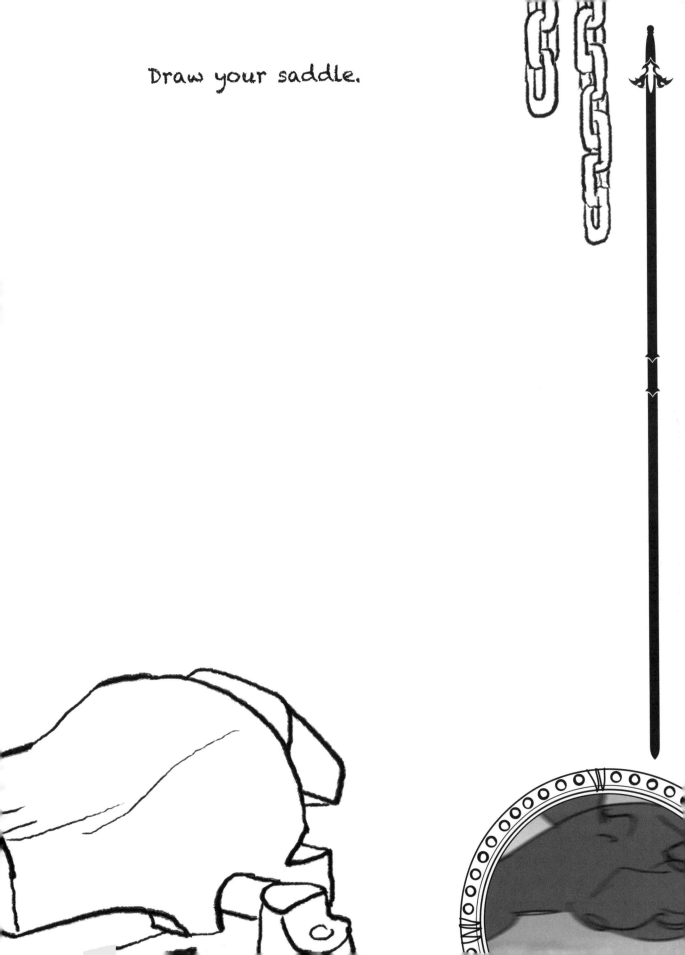

Gobber's dragon likes to sleep on the job.

What is he dreaming about?

Your dragon has a toothache and
Gobber removes the sore tooth!

Draw the rest of
the dragon teeth.

It's time to wash your dragon
after the Dragon Race.

Draw as many soap bubbles as you can.

This Viking needs a beard.

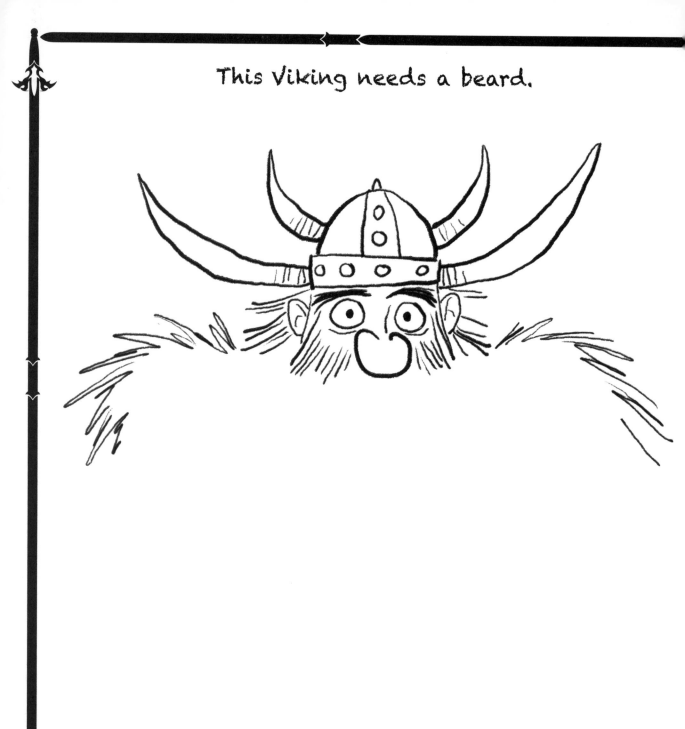

This Viking needs a helmet.

Hiccup tells Stoick that Drago is coming to Berk to steal all the dragons!

Stoick is scared. He says no one can leave Berk.

Hiccup makes a plan to escape before Stoick closes the gates.

Hiccup gathers supplies for the long fight to Drago's.

Astrid runs after Hiccup. "Stoick said it's not safe!"

Hiccup jumps on Toothless's back. "I have to stop Drago."

Hiccup and Toothless are flying. The gates are closing fast . . .

. . . they make it through just as the wooden doors shut!

Toothless and Hiccup have a long flight ahead, but they are ready to stop Drago and his dragon army!

Gobber makes all the dragon saddles at his workshop. He has every tool he needs.

Draw a new tool for Gobber.

Toothless likes to lick Hiccup with his big, slobbery tongue. Draw Hiccup's hair sticking up.

Before you fly, you need lots of supplies. What do you pack?

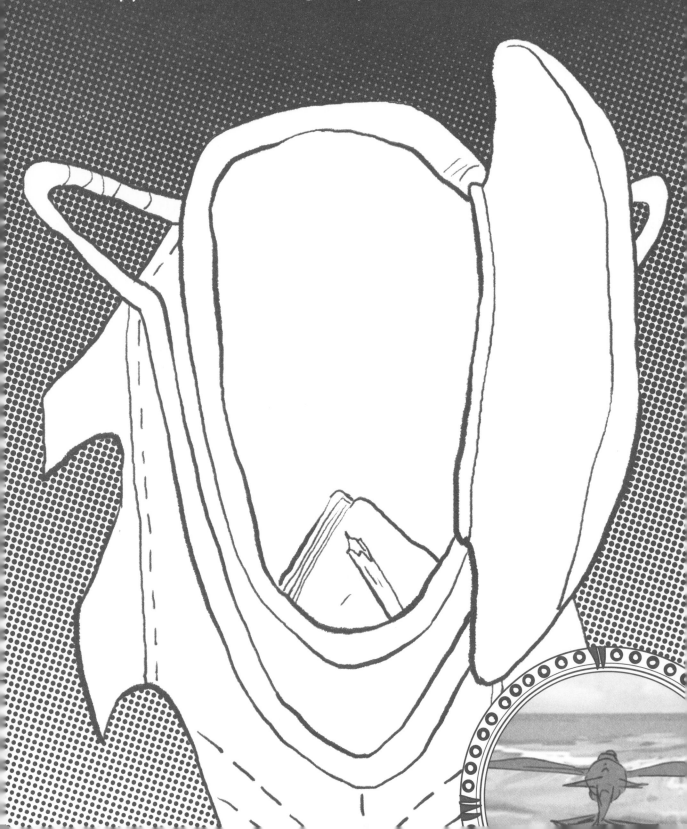

Hiccup invented a special suit so he and Toothless can fly next to each other.

Draw their wings.

Dragon riders like to fly through the clouds.
Some of the clouds are shaped like objects.

Fill the sky with shaped clouds.

The Vikings need their shields before they can battle Drago and the rest of his dragon army.

Draw shields for the people of Berk.

You aren't the only ones in the sky.

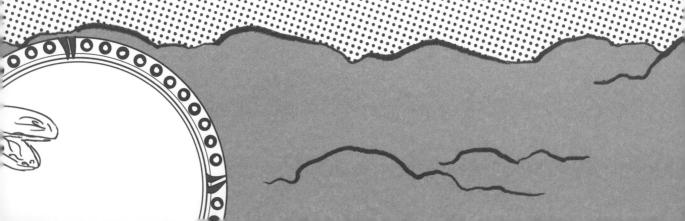

What else is flying near you?

Oh no! A mountain appears out of the fog.

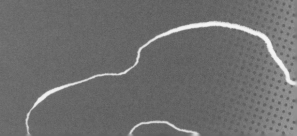

Draw the mountain.

Clouds are a good way to send a message to people below.

Draw a message using clouds.

There are big, dark clouds in the sky—
time to head back to Berk.

Draw a storm.

Stormfly is Astrid's dragon,
and she loves to play fetch.

What else did Stormfly fetch?

Eret is a professional dragon trapper. He's always thinking of new ways to find and trap dragons.

Draw a trap.

The Vikings set sail on their longboats.
The village looks so small from far away.

Draw your view of Berk.

The Vikings spend a lot of time fishing.

Draw what they caught.

Hiccup is picked up by a dragon and flown to a mysterious ice nest. You've never seen anything like it!

Draw the ice nest.

Oh look! The dragon eggs are hatching.

Draw the baby dragons.

Valka saves many different dragons. Hiccup has never seen some of these dragons!

Draw scales on all the dragons.

The Bewilderbeast, the biggest dragon Hiccup has ever seen, says hello by blowing icy cool air into his face.

Draw icicles hanging off of Hiccup.

It's been a long day of flying your dragon.
Draw a sunset.

Hiccup wears a mask when he rides Toothless.
Draw a mask for Hiccup.

Dragons love to eat fish, and they can eat a lot!

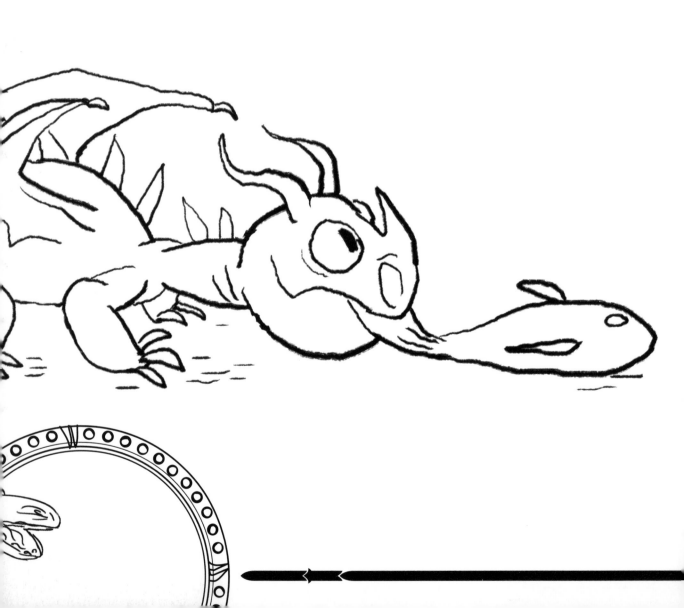

Draw a pile of fish for your hungry dragon.

Hiccup is surrounded by dragons. He communicates with them using his dragon blade.

Draw fire on the dragon blade.

The baby dragons don't listen to the Bewilderbeast and are always causing mischief.

What are the baby dragons fighting over?

Toothless likes to pick up a big stick
with his mouth and draw in the snow.

What did Toothless draw?

The Bewilderbeast dives into the ocean and shoots fish up into the air for all the other dragons to eat. It's raining fish!

Draw the fish.

You and Fishlegs find a new dragon.

Design its trading card.

Valka holds a tall, wooden staff. She uses it to communicate with the dragons.

Draw your own dragon staff.

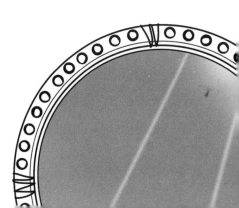

Gobber is cooking a delicious dinner over the fire.

What is Gobber cooking?

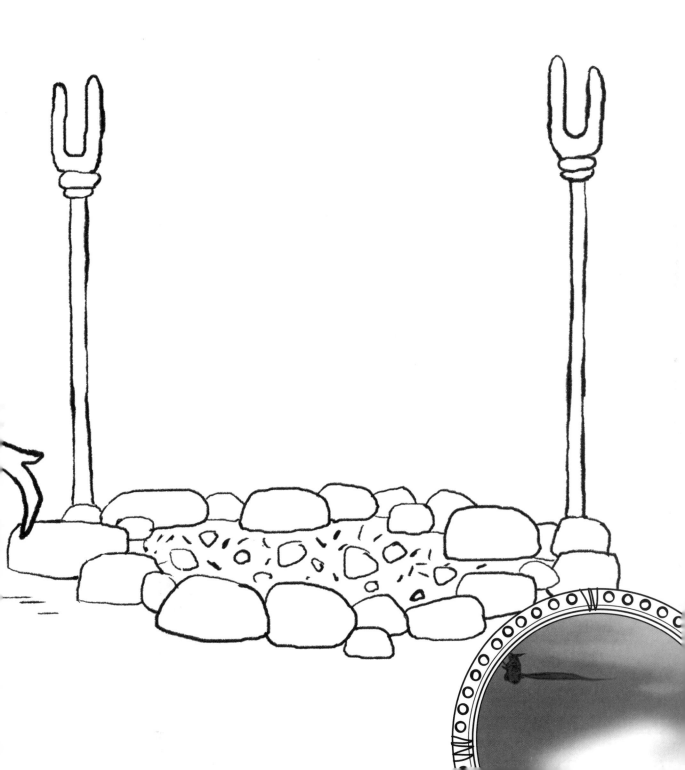

Grump uses his big, round
tail to knock things over.

Draw what Grump knocks over.

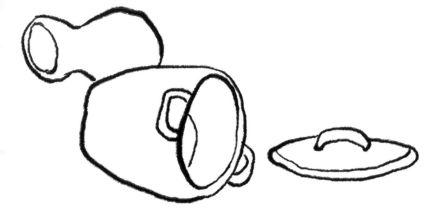

Toothless is hiding under
Cloudjumper's large wing.

What else is hiding under Cloudjumper's wing?

Hiccup, Valka, and Stoick are ready to go back to Berk as a family.

Draw your family as Vikings.

Hiccup discovers new dragons when he explores with Toothless. Some are short, but one is really long.

Draw an even longer dragon.

Some dragons shoot ice and some shoot fire. The Thunderdrum shoots a sonic blast. Draw the sonic blast.

Stormfly shoots spikes. Draw flying spikes.

The Whispering Death can travel
for miles through the dirt.

Draw the Whispering Death's underground path.

Drago wears a heavy cape that protects him from the dragon's fiery blast.

Draw the dragon's fire.

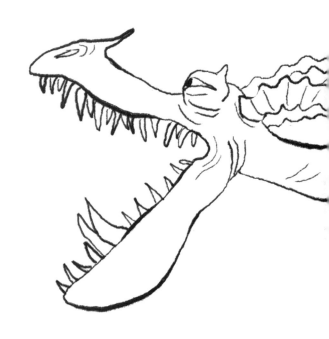

Astrid and the rest of the gang find Drago's dragon army. They are amazed by what they see from the snowy cliff.

Draw a dragon army.

The Bewilderbeast is the biggest
dragon the Vikings have ever seen.

Draw a bunch of tiny dragons.

All the dragons have been
hypnotized by the alpha dragon.

Draw their eyes.

Drago's men have kidnapped Astrid
and the rest of the Viking gang, and
brought them onto Drago's boat.

Finish Drago's boat.

Hiccup's friends try to distract the Bewilderbeast with sheep, but one gets stuck in the spikes!

Finish drawing the Bewilderbeast's spikes.

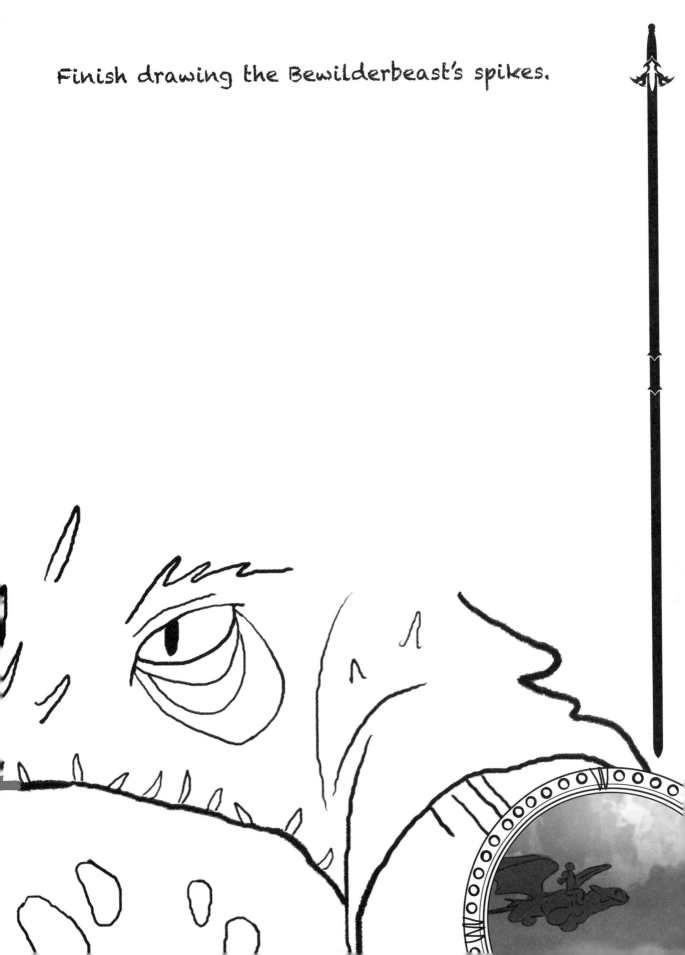

Toothless blasts the ice away and saves Hiccup!

Draw the exploding ice.

Finish the doors and decorate the beams.

Draw your house in Berk.

You saved the day with Hiccup and Toothless.

Draw the Viking's celebration.

The adventure continues...
Where do you fly next?